LETTING GO

A STORY ABOUT LOSING, AND FINDING, ONE'S WINGS

WRITTEN AND ILLUSTRATED BY ANDY BOERGER

PUBLISHED BY
TED E BEANS
(A-LI'L DIVISION OF INKNBEANS PRESS)
©2014

Cover art: Andy Boerger

© 2014   Andy Boerger and Ted E Beans (a li'l division of Inknbeans Press)

ISBN-13: 978-0692233450 (Ted E Beans)

ISBN-10: 0692233458

For MM

This story came to me one afternoon as I walked along the river near my home. First, it wasn't there. And then it was.

But, as soon as it just sort of popped into my head, I knew that it was a representation of all the many things that had happened in my life, and specifically the many times I found it difficult to let go of something long after it was time to. So, this book is dedicated to every person who, for whatever reason, finds it hard to let go.

My wish is that it will pop into each reader's life at a time when it can lend the most encouragement.

ONCE...

... THERE WAS A VERY SMALL,
BUT VERY SKILLED, PILOT.

In his shiny, tiny plane,
he climbed so high,
and called the sky his home.

HE WAS JOYFUL, HAPPY
AND
FREEEEEEEEEEEEEEEEEE!

LIKE HIS BEST FRIENDS,
THE BIRDS.

UNTIL ONE DAY...

...WHEN SOMETHING BAD HAPPENED.

SOMETHING REALLY BAD

THAT WAS NOT HIS FAULT!

The sky no longer felt
like home, as he
fell through it
like a stone.

AS HE PLUNGED DOWNWARD
HE SAW SOMETHING
RUSHING TO MEET HIM.

HE GRABBED OUT, INSTICTIVELY;
A BRANCH!

He was saved!
He held on for dear life
and did not look down!

HE COULDN'T SEE HIGH UP ENOUGH ABOVE THE BRANCH TO KNOW IF ANYONE WAS THERE BEYOND THE EDGE, BUT HE CLEARED HIS THROAT, AND SCREAMED!

"HEEEELLLLPP!"

NOBODY ANSWERED.

Things got worse for the little pilot. Gradually, he realized that there was something funny about the bark of the branch he was holding onto.

It seemed to have some kind of poison on its surface that made his skin crawl.

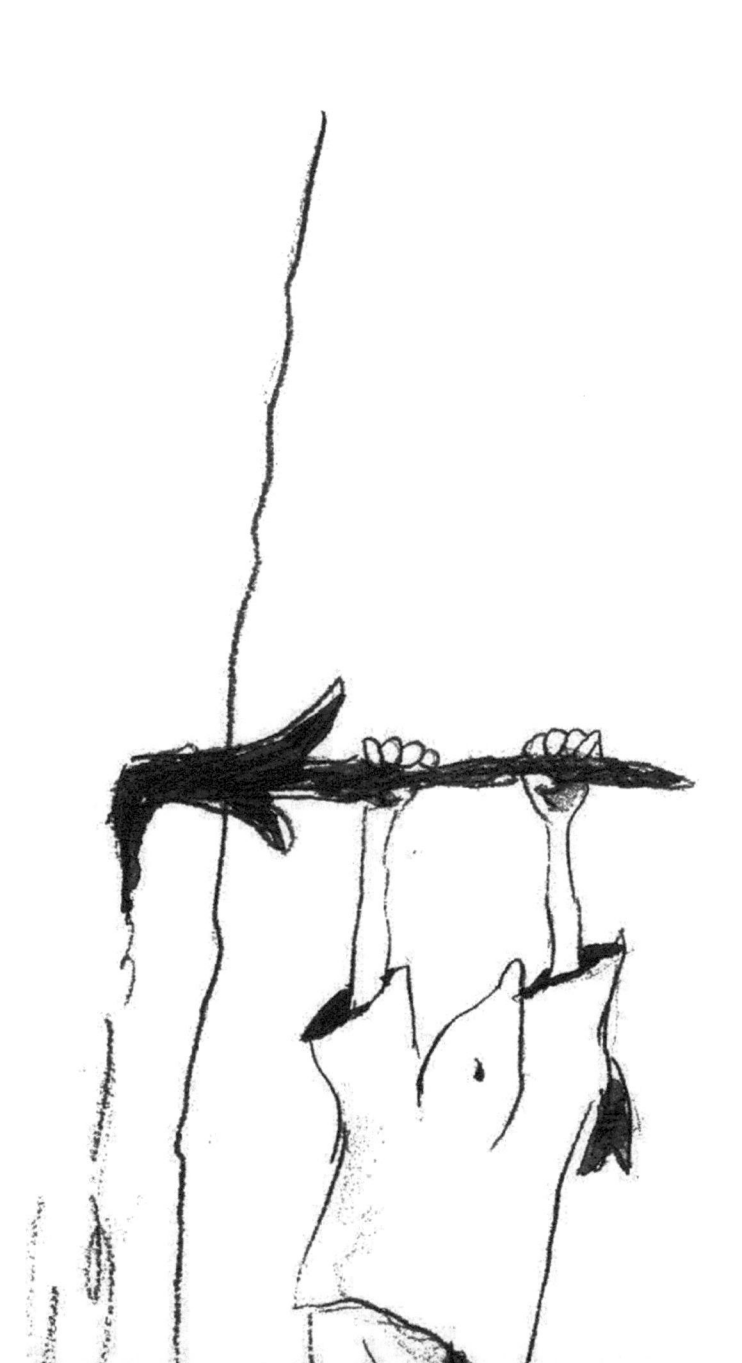

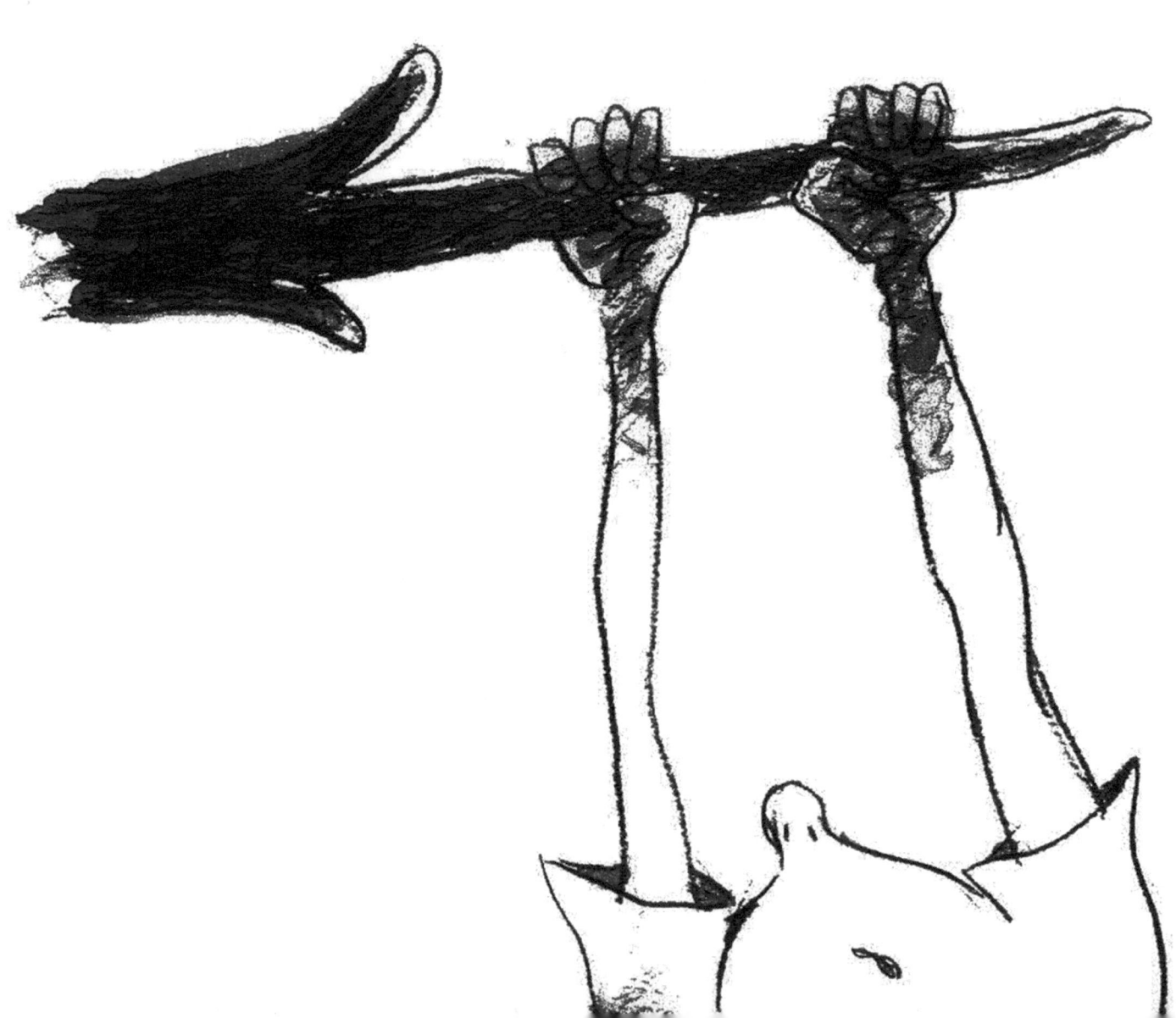

The longer he held onto the branch,
the stranger and more uncomfortable
he felt.
He felt the poison on the branch
seeping into his bloodstream.
He could feel it weakening him.

THIS WAS SOMETHING
HE HAD NEVER EVEN
THOUGHT ABOUT
BEFORE.

HE BECAME TERRIFIED.

HE SCREAMED, WITH THE
LAST GASPS OF BREATH INSIDE HIM
TO ANYBODY,
OR TO NOBODY....

"HEEEELLLLLLLLLLLPPPP!!!!"
"ISN'T ANYBODY OUT THERE?!"
"WHY WON'T ANYBODY SAVE ME??"

AS BEFORE, NO ONE ANSWERED.

THE BOY LOST ALL HOPE, ALL
STRENTH AND ALL FAITH.
HE WAS ALONE IN THE UNIVERSE,
AND NOBODY CARED
IF HE LIVED OR DIED.
HE FELT HIS FINGERS WEAKEN
AROUND THE POISONOUS
BRANCH.
HECOULDN'T HOLD ON
ANY LONGER

HE LET GO.

AND FELL TO WHAT WAS WAITING BELOW.

AMONG HIS FRIENDS, THE BOY
QUICKLY REGAINED HIS STRENGTH.
THEN, SUDDENLY, HE, SOMEHOW KNEW
THAT THERE WAS SOMETHING HE COULD DO!

THE WINGS HE THOUGHT
HE'D LOST THAT DAY

HADN'T REALLY GONE AWAY.

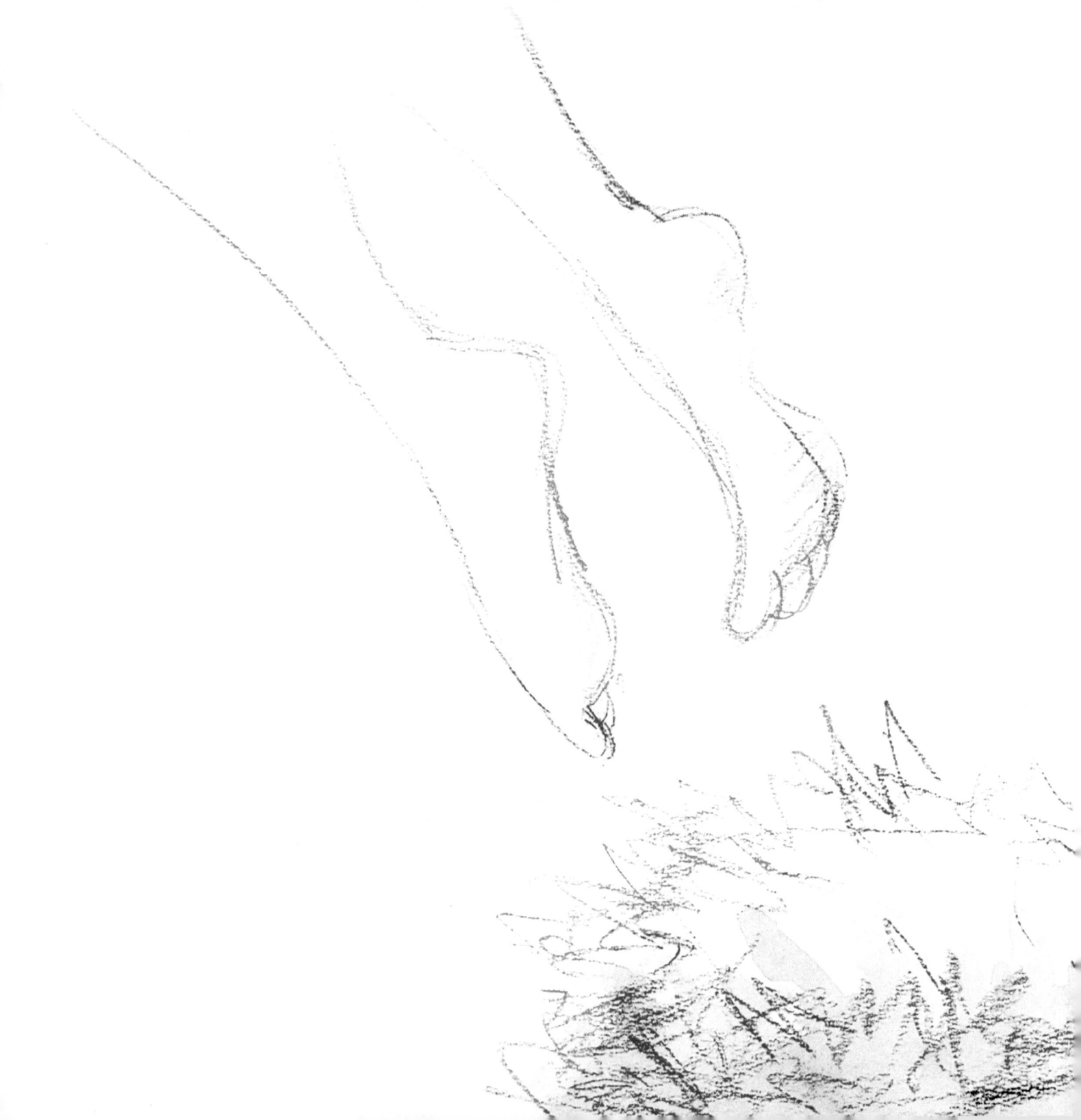

AND SO, WE COME TO THE END
OF THE STORY ABOUT
A LITTLE PILOT, WHO
LOST A GREAT DEAL,
AND GAINED SO MUCH MORE.

THE END

About the Author

I'm an illustrator/writer/educator from Columbus, Ohio. I have lived in Tokyo for the past twenty odd years. I've worn many hats throughout that time, though. Everything I've done ties into my passion for communicating and creating. Combining words with images is a particular passion of mine. And children and animals are two of my favourite subjects for drawing, especially when the two interact in revealing ways.

My illustrations appear in *Sherlock Ferret and the Missing Necklace*, *Sherlock Ferret and the Multiplying Masterpieces* (with a third in the series, already in the works), and *Without My Boswell*, each written by Hugh Ashton, my previous book, *I Like You More Each Day*, all published by Ted E Beans (a li'l division of Inknbeans Press), as well as *What Does the Tooth Fairy Do with Our Teeth?* by Denise Barry. Follow my blog at andysart-andyboerger.blogspot.jp. There's something for almost everyone there.

Andy Boerger

Also Available from Ted E Beans
(a li'l division of Inknbeans Press)

The Open Pillow, David Rowinski and Dea Lenihan
Digweed, the Cat, Eric Pullin
In My Sister's World, Ey Wade
The Magical Tree, Eric Pullin
A Thin Wisp of Smoke, Eric Pullin
The Travis Tales, Rose Salsman and Claire Turtlemoon
Dabby and Maxie, Robin Bee Owens
The Swamp Fairy, Robin Bee Owens
Sherlock Ferret and the Missing Necklace, Hugh Ashton and Andy Boerger
Sherlock Ferret and the Multiplying Masterpieces, Hugh Ashton and Andy Boerger
I Like You More Each Day, Andy Boerger
Torhjean, No! series, Jackie Williams
Liam and Storm's Alien Adventures, Jackie Williams
Read With Me, Pops series, Pops Burkett
God's Pinky Promises, Dawn Hood

Ted E Beans
a li'l division of
Inknbeans Press

www.ingramcontent.com/pod-product-compliance
Lightning Source LLC
Chambersburg PA
CBHW040959170626
46815CB00002B/70